Ascension Lutheran Church and School
8811 St. Joe Road
Fort Wayne, IN 46835
260-486-2226

# Iris and Walter
## and the
## Substitute Teacher

# Iris and Walter
## and the Substitute Teacher

WRITTEN BY
Elissa Haden Guest

ILLUSTRATED BY
Christine Davenier

GULLIVER BOOKS
HARCOURT, INC.

ORLANDO AUSTIN NEW YORK
SAN DIEGO TORONTO LONDON

For Liz Van Doren—E. H. G.

To Isabelle Davenier, the teacher all kids should have—C. D.

Text copyright © 2004 by Elissa Haden Guest
Illustrations copyright © 2004 by Christine Davenier

All rights reserved. No part of this publication may be reproduced or transmitted in any form or by any means, electronic or mechanical, including photocopy, recording, or any information storage and retrieval system, without permission in writing from the publisher.

Requests for permission to make copies of any part of the work should be mailed to the following address: Permissions Department, Harcourt, Inc., 6277 Sea Harbor Drive, Orlando, Florida 32887-6777.

www.HarcourtBooks.com

*Gulliver Books* is a trademark of Harcourt, Inc., registered in the United States of America and/or other jurisdictions.

Library of Congress Cataloging-in-Publication Data
Guest, Elissa Haden.
Iris and Walter and the substitute teacher/written by Elissa Haden Guest; illustrated by Christine Davenier.
p. cm.
"Gulliver Books."
Summary: When Iris's grandfather comes to her school as a substitute teacher, she has a hard time sharing him with the other students.
[1. Teachers—Fiction. 2. Grandfathers—Fiction. 3. Jealousy—Fiction. 4. Schools—Fiction.] I. Davenier, Christine, ill. II. Title.
PZ7.G9375Isl 2004
[E]—dc22 2003013524
ISBN 0-15-205013-2

First edition

H G F E D C B A

Manufactured in China

# Contents

1. A Surprise 6

2. The Special Helper 14

3. Misery 22

4. Ice Cream 36

12
3
6

# 1. A Surprise

Iris loved school.
She loved her sunny classroom.
She loved learning how to tell time.
She loved trading lunches with her best friend, Walter.
And oh, how Iris loved Miss Cherry.

In the afternoons, when Iris and Grandpa
walked home from school, Iris told Grandpa
all about school and Miss Cherry.
And Grandpa told Iris stories
about when he had been a teacher.

One morning, when Iris arrived at school,
the principal was in the room.
"Did you hear the news?" asked Walter.
"What?" asked Iris.

"Miss Cherry is sick," said Benny.

"We're getting a substitute," said Walter.

"A substitute!" said Iris.

They had never had a substitute before.

Just then, the principal said,
"Good morning, boys and girls.
Today you are having a substitute teacher.

I am sure you will all listen to him
and be on your best behavior."
The door opened…and in came Grandpa!

# 2. The Special Helper

"Grandpa, what are you doing here?" asked Iris.
"The regular substitute could not come, so I'm going to be the teacher today," said Grandpa.
Iris was so excited.
Her grandpa was going to teach the class!
"Iris, why don't you be the special helper today," said the principal.
"Oh boy!" said Iris.

Iris sat next to Grandpa while he told the class a wonderful story.

She erased the chalkboard after spelling.

Iris showed Grandpa where Miss Cherry kept the paint for art.

And at snack time, Iris and Walter passed out the apples.

When the bell rang, Iris said,
"Grandpa, that's the bell for recess."
"Oh no, it's raining," said Benny.
"Now we can't go outside," said Walter.

"Well then, it's the perfect day
for musical chairs," said Grandpa.
The children played one game
and then another.
"Your grandpa is so much fun," said Benny.
"He sure is," said Lulu.
Iris was so proud.

After school, the principal asked Grandpa if he could teach the class again the next day.
"Certainly," said Grandpa.
"Hooray!" said Walter.

On the way home, Iris said, "Grandpa, you're a great teacher."
"And you, my girl, are a great helper," said Grandpa.

"Guess what, Rosie?" said Iris that night. "*I* was Grandpa's helper today. It was so much fun! I can't wait for tomorrow."

# 3. Misery

The next morning, everyone was excited to see Grandpa again.

"Are you going to tell us another story?" asked Benny.

"This morning I'd like someone to tell *me* a story," said Grandpa.

All the children raised their hands.

Iris was sure Grandpa was going to pick her.
But Grandpa picked Benny.

At snack time, Jenny asked Grandpa,
"May I pass out the crackers today?"
"Of course," said Grandpa.
*But I'm the helper,* thought Iris.

At lunch, Iris wanted to sit next to Grandpa.
But Grandpa never sat down.
He was too busy.

Benny needed a Band-Aid.
Lulu lost her sweater.
And Jenny had left her
lunch bag at home.

In the afternoon, Grandpa said,
"Let's go for a walk. Everyone can find something interesting to give Miss Cherry tomorrow."
Benny and Jenny rushed to hold Grandpa's hands.
*He's my grandpa*, thought Iris.

"Iris, what are you going to give Miss Cherry?"
asked Walter.
"I don't know," said Iris.
"Do you want to give her this leaf?"
asked Walter.
"No," said Iris, and she walked away.

Back at school, Lulu said,
"Look at the rock I found."
"I found a leaf," said Walter.

"Iris, what did you find for Miss Cherry?"
asked Grandpa.
"Nothing!" said Iris.

"Why doesn't everyone make a card
for Miss Cherry," said Grandpa.
While everyone was drawing,
Grandpa went over to Iris.
"Iris, what's wrong?" he whispered.
"Everything," said Iris. "I didn't get to tell a
story. I didn't get to pass out the snack.
I didn't find anything for Miss Cherry. And…"
"And what, my girl?" Grandpa asked.

How could Iris tell Grandpa that she didn't want him to be the teacher anymore? She just wanted him to be Grandpa.

"Iris, is it hard having me be your teacher?" asked Grandpa.

"Really hard," said Iris.

"I understand, but school is almost over," said Grandpa.

# 4. Ice Cream

On the way home from school, Grandpa said,
"This was not an easy day, was it?"
"No," said Iris.
"But we got through it," said Grandpa.
"I think we should celebrate."
"Oh yes!" said Iris.

Iris and Grandpa went to
the Rainbow Café.
They sat on their favorite stools.
They ordered their favorite ice cream.

Iris had a vanilla ice-cream sundae with chocolate syrup and whipped cream. Grandpa had a strawberry ice-cream cone.

"Delicious," said Iris.
"Superb," said Grandpa.
They ate every last bite.

On the way home, Iris found
just the right present
for Miss Cherry.

The next morning,
Iris could not wait for the day to begin.
Miss Cherry was back.
Walter was waiting.

And, best of all,
Grandpa was her grandpa again.

The illustrations in this book were created in pen-and-ink on keacolor paper.
The display type was set in Elroy.
The text type was set in Fairfield Medium.
Color separations by Bright Arts Ltd., Hong Kong
Manufactured by South China Printing Company, Ltd., China
This book was printed on totally chlorine-free Stora Enso Matte paper.
Production supervision by Sandra Grebenar and Wendi Taylor
Designed by Lydia D'moch and Suzanne Fridley

TALCS00021835X